Karen's School Bus

Look for these
and other books about Karen
in the
Baby-sitters Little Sister series

# 1 Karen's Witch	#33 Karen's Secret
# 2 Karen's Roller Skates	#34 Karen's Snow Day
# 3 Karen's Worst Day	#35 Karen's Doll Hospital
# 4 Karen's Kittycat Club	#36 Karen's New Friend
# 5 Karen's School Picture	#37 Karen's Tuba
# 6 Karen's Little Sister	#38 Karen's Big Lie
# 7 Karen's Birthday	#39 Karen's Wedding
# 8 Karen's Haircut	#40 Karen's Newspaper
# 9 Karen's Sleepover	#41 Karen's School
#10 Karen's Grandmothers	#42 Karen's Pizza Party
#11 Karen's Prize	#43 Karen's Toothache
#12 Karen's Ghost	#44 Karen's Big Weekend
#13 Karen's Surprise	#45 Karen's Twin
#14 Karen's New Year	#46 Karen's Baby-sitter
#15 Karen's in Love	#47 Karen's Kite
#16 Karen's Goldfish	#48 Karen's Two Families
#17 Karen's Brothers	#49 Karen's Stepmother
#18 Karen's Home Run	#50 Karen's Lucky Penny
#19 Karen's Good-bye	#51 Karen's Big Top
#20 Karen's Carnival	#52 Karen's Mermaid
#21 Karen's New Teacher	#53 Karen's School Bus
#22 Karen's Little Witch	#54 Karen's Candy
#23 Karen's Doll	
#24 Karen's School Trip	Super Specials:
#25 Karen's Pen Pal	# 1 Karen's Wish
#26 Karen's Ducklings	# 2 Karen's Plane Trip
#27 Karen's Big Joke	# 3 Karen's Mystery
#28 Karen's Tea Party	# 4 Karen, Hannie, and
#29 Karen's Cartwheel	Nancy: The Three
#30 Karen's Kittens	Musketeers
#31 Karen's Bully	# 5 Karen's Baby
#32 Karen's Pumpkin Patch	# 6 Karen's Campout

BABY-SITTERS
Little Sister

Karen's School Bus
Ann M. Martin

Illustrations by Susan Tang

A
LITTLE APPLE
PAPERBACK

SCHOLASTIC INC.
New York Toronto London Auckland Sydney

No part of this publication may be reproduced in whole or in part, or stored in a retrieval system, or transmitted in any form or by any means, electronic, mechanical, photocopying, recording, or otherwise, without written permission of the publisher. For information regarding permission, write to Scholastic Inc., 555 Broadway, New York, NY 10012.

ISBN 0-590-48300-5

12 11 10 9 8 7 6 5 4 3 2 1   4 5 6 7 8 9/9

Printed in the U.S.A.   40

First Scholastic printing, September 1994

The author gratefully acknowledges
Stephanie Calmenson
for her help
with this book.

Karen's School Bus

September Saturday

Ding-dong!

"I will get it!" I said.

I raced out of my room and down the stairs of the big house. I already knew who was at the door. It was my friend, Hannie.

"Hi, Karen! Are you ready to go?" said Hannie.

We were going skating in the neighborhood.

"I have to get my skates. I will be right back," I said.

It was a September Saturday morning.

September is one of my favorite months. When September comes, school starts. I love school. As soon as September is over, it is October. That means it is Halloween. I love Halloween. November and Thanksgiving come next. Did you know I love Thanksgiving? Then comes December. And Christmas. You guessed it. I *love* Christmas. I love lots of things.

My name is Karen Brewer. I am seven years old. I have blonde hair, blue eyes, and a bunch of freckles. Oh, yes. I wear glasses. I have two pairs. I wear my blue pair when I am reading. I wear my pink pair the rest of the time. (I do not wear them in the bathtub, or when I am sleeping.)

I got my skates out of my closet. It was bright and sunny. It was a perfect roller-skating day.

On my way back downstairs, I bumped into Emily Michelle. She is my little sister. She is two and a half.

"Whee!" said Emily. She says that whenever she sees roller skates.

I let her spin the wheels a few times with her fingers.

"Whee!" she said again.

"I have to go, Emily. Hannie is waiting for me," I said.

I was halfway downstairs when I bumped into Andrew. He is my little brother. He is four going on five.

"I want to go roller skating, too," he said.

"Sorry," I replied. "I am going with Hannie."

"Beep, beep! You are blocking the stairs," called my stepbrother, David Michael. He whizzed by us.

Then Daddy poked his head out of his room.

"Why don't you invite Hannie back here for lunch after you skate?" he said.

"Thanks, Daddy. I will," I replied.

By the time I got back down to Hannie, I had seen almost everybody in my big-house family. That was a lot of people! I had also tripped over our puppy and almost stomped on our cat's tail.

Hannie was waiting for me outside. She was skating back and forth in front of my house.

"What took you so long?" she asked.

"You know my big-house family," I said. "You cannot get out the door without something going on. That is because there are so many people."

My big-house family is not the only family I have either. I have another one. I will tell you all about it.

Karen's Cool Families

When I was little, the big house was my only house. I lived there with Mommy, Daddy, and Andrew. It was a big house with a little family.

Then Mommy and Daddy started fighting a lot. They explained to Andrew and me that the fights had nothing to do with us. They loved both of us very much. But Mommy and Daddy could not get along with each other anymore. So they got a divorce.

Mommy moved out of the big house with

Andrew and me. We moved to a little house not too far away in Stoneybrook, Connecticut. Then Mommy met a nice man named Seth Engle. Mommy and Seth got married. So now Seth is my stepfather. Every other month Andrew and I live in the little house with Mommy, Seth, Midgie (Seth's dog), Rocky (Seth's cat), Emily Junior (my pet rat), and Bob (Andrew's hermit crab).

Daddy stayed in the big house. It is the house he grew up in. He met somebody nice, too. Her name is Elizabeth Thomas. Daddy and Elizabeth got married. So now Elizabeth is my stepmother. She was married before and had four children, who are my stepbrothers and stepsister. They are Sam and Charlie, who are so old they are in high school; David Michael, who is seven, like me; and Kristy, who is thirteen and the best stepsister ever.

Then there is Emily Michelle. I already told you that she is two and a half. But I did not tell you that she was adopted from a faraway country called Vietnam. (She is very cute. That is why I named my pet rat after her.)

Nannie lives at the big house, too. She is Elizabeth's mother. That makes her my stepgrandmother. She came to live with us so she could help take care of Emily. But really she helps take care of everyone.

The puppy I tripped over is a big, floppy Bernese mountain dog named Shannon. The cat I almost stomped on is a grouchy old tiger cat named Boo-Boo. (If I had stomped on his tail he would have had a *real* boo-boo!) Then there are two goldfish. Crystal Light the Second belongs to me. Goldfishie belongs to Andrew. The last two pets at the big house are my rat, Emily Junior, and Andrew's hermit crab, Bob. They go wherever we go.

Guess what. I have a special name for Andrew and me. I call us Andrew Two-Two and Karen Two-Two. (I got that idea when my teacher read a book to our class called, *Jacob Two-Two Meets the Hooded Fang*.) I call us two-twos because we have two of so many things. We have two houses and two families. We have two sets of clothes and toys and books, one at each house. I have two stuffed cats. (Goosie is my little-house cat. Moosie is my big-house cat.) And I have two pieces of Tickly, my special blanket. (I only have one pair of roller skates, though. It is a good thing I remembered to bring them to the big house. Otherwise I could not have skated with Hannie.)

I also have two best friends. Hannie Papadakis lives across the street and one house down from Daddy's house. Nancy Dawes lives next door to Mommy's house.

Sometimes it is hard being a two-two. I miss Mommy when I am with Daddy. And I miss Daddy when I am with Mommy. But those are my families. Most of the time I think they are pretty cool.

See You at the Bus Stop

"*The wheels on the bus go round and round all over town!*"

"*Ninety-nine bottles of pop on the wall. Ninety-nine bottles of pop! If one of those bottles should happen to fall, ninety-eight bottles of pop on the wall!*"

It was Sunday. Hannie and I were up in my room singing every bus song we knew. That was because tomorrow we were going to school a special new way.

The name of my school is Stoneybrook Academy. Hannie, Nancy, and I go there together. We are even in the same class. (We do almost everything together. That is why we call ourselves the Three Musketeers.)

Our teacher's name is Ms. Colman. She is a very excellent teacher. She always makes our lessons interesting and fun. And she hardly ever yells. Sometimes I call out in class when I am not supposed to. But Ms. Colman does not get angry. She just reminds me to use my indoor voice and to raise my hand.

Last week Ms. Colman made a Surprising Announcement. (Those are my favorite kind.) She told us that anyone who lived a certain distance from school would get to ride on the new school buses.

"We are so lucky," said Hannie now, when we had stopped singing bus songs. "If we lived one block closer to school, we could not ride on the bus."

"I am double lucky," I said. "*Both* my houses are far enough away. I will ride with you when I live at the big house. I will ride with Nancy when I live at the little house."

"I wish the Three Musketeers could ride together. That would be triple fun," said Hannie.

"I know. We had fun on the bus when we went to sleepaway camp," I replied.

"And we always have fun when we go on a bus for a class trip," said Hannie.

"Except the time we went to the airport," I said. "Remember how Natalie almost got sick? And some of the kids made fun of her."

"Poor Natalie. I am glad I do not get bus sick," said Hannie.

"Me too," I replied. "Hey, I have an idea. We can make believe we are Lovely Ladies on a bus in Paris. *Oui, ma chérie?*"

"What did you say?" asked Hannie.

"I said 'Yes, my dear' in French. Sam taught me that. He is learning French in high school," I said.

"We make believe we are going to Paris all the time," said Hannie. "Let's go somewhere else."

"How about New York City?" I said. "I can be a French tourist. *Oui, oui?*"

"*Sí, señorita,*" said Hannie. "That means 'yes, miss,' in Spanish. I will be a tourist from Spain."

Just then, Daddy knocked on our door.

"Sorry to break up the party, girls. But it is almost five o'clock," said Daddy.

"Wow, I have got to get home," said Hannie. "This day went so fast. We had fun!"

"And we will have fun tomorrow on our new school bus," I said. "See you at the bus stop."

"*Sí, sí,*" said Hannie.

"*Oui, oui!*" I replied.

Ew, Gross!

It was Monday. Bus day!

I put on my favorite outfit in honor of my first school bus ride. This is what I wore: black leggings, yellow socks, black sneakers, yellow taxi cab sweater. (I would have worn a school bus sweater. But I did not have one. I hoped this would not hurt the bus driver's feelings.)

The bus stop was just down the street. I walked there by myself. Hannie and her brother, Linny, were waiting with a few other kids from our block. Linny is David Michael's friend.

"Hi, everyone!" I called.

I was gigundoly excited about my first school bus morning.

"Hey, listen to this joke," I said. "Why didn't the boy take the school bus home?"

"I don't know," said Hannie. "Why?"

"Because his mother would just make him take it back!" I said.

I laughed loudly. I knew the joke was not so funny. But I had nervous butterflies in my stomach. Laughing made me feel better.

"Here comes the bus!" said Linny.

A big yellow bus was coming toward us. The front of the bus looked like a face with headlights for eyes. I was glad it was a friendly face.

I stood up tall. There were going to be kids in every grade from kindergarten to sixth on the bus. I did not want to look like a baby.

The bus pulled up to the curb. *Swish*. The doors flew open.

"You go first," I whispered to Linny.

He bounced up the steps. Hannie and I looked at each other.

"Ready?" I said.

"Ready," said Hannie.

We held hands and climbed onto the bus. It was more than half filled. The oldest kids were sitting at the back.

Linny had found a seat in the middle of the bus next to his pal, Bart Cole.

"Hi, Karen. Hi, Hannie," called Liddie Yuan.

Liddie was sitting next to Edwin. They are in Mr. Berger's class. Mr. Berger is the other second-grade teacher. His class is next door to Ms. Colman's.

Hannie and I slid into two seats at the front with the other kids our age.

Swish. The doors closed and the bus started down the street.

Bump. *Bump-bump*. The bus felt very bouncy. Maybe it was the butterflies in my

16

stomach. Maybe I had eaten too much breakfast. Maybe . . .

Uh-oh. It was a good thing I had the aisle seat. Before I knew what was happening, I had thrown up all over the place.

"Ew, gross!" called a voice from the back.

"Are you okay, Karen?" said Hannie. She put her hand on my shoulder.

I nodded. I felt embarrassed. At least I did not feel sick anymore.

"I don't see why we have to ride the bus with babies," said the voice from the back.

"Hadley Smith you are being mean," said a second voice.

"Well, it is gross," said the girl named Hadley.

I turned around quickly. The girl named Hadley was holding her nose.

I wished the bus would get to school fast.

A Day at Home

As soon as I got to school, I was sent to see Mrs. Pazden. She is the school nurse.

"I am perfectly fine," I said.

"I am glad you feel better, Karen," said Mrs. Pazden. "But you look a little pale. And your skin feels clammy."

Butterflies in my stomach. Clams on my skin. I was a walking zoo.

Mrs. Pazden called the big house. Nannie came to pick me up in the Pink Clinker. (That is the name of Nannie's car.) She had Emily with her.

"I feel fine," I said to Nannie. "Really I do."

"You do look pale," said Nannie. "A day at home will be good for you."

Guess what. It was. I had a lot to keep me busy. I played with Moosie. I fed Crystal Light. I cleaned Emily Junior's cage. And I was a very good helper for Nannie. Mainly I watched Emily while Nannie did things around the house.

"There is no school for me today. But that does not mean that you cannot go to school," I said. "Miss Karen's School is now in session."

I once had a school for Andrew and some other little kids in the neighborhood. I started out being very strict. No one had a good time. So I decided to be a nice teacher like Ms. Colman. Then school was fun.

" 'Tory time?" said Emily.

"Sure it is story time," I said. "What story would you like to hear?"

Emily went to the bookcase and pulled out *Millions of Cats*.

"That is a good one," I said.

When I finished reading I took out paper and crayons. While Emily scribbled, I drew lots of cats all over the page. (Maybe Emily was drawing cats, too. But they looked like scribbles to me.)

By lunchtime, I had forgotten about getting sick in the morning. Nannie made soup and tuna fish sandwiches. I ate every bite.

"Can we make butterscotch pudding?" I asked. "Then everyone can have it for dessert at dinner."

I love to make pudding. These are my jobs: Measuring and pouring the milk. Stirring the pudding. Licking the pot. (That is my favorite part.)

Emily and I played school again after lunch. When we finished, I went to call Hannie. I wanted to make sure everyone at school missed me. And I wanted to hear all about the bus ride home.

"Hi, Hannie!" I said.

Hannie asked me if I was feeling better.

When I said I was, she told me about the bus ride home.

The butterflies started coming back. Little baby ones. That is because on the bus ride home, the big kids were still talking about how I threw up. Hannie said that girl Hadley was doing most of the talking.

"That is okay," I said to Hannie. "They will forget all about it by tomorrow."

I hoped I was right.

Ms. Colman's Class

On Tuesday, I almost missed the bus. I had to run down the block to make it in time.

That is because I ran back to get my Little Mermaid sunglasses. I hoped the kids on the bus would not recognize me when I had them on.

"Watch out! Here comes Barf-Face!" called Hadley from the back of the bus.

I guess the glasses did not work. They started teasing Hannie next. Only not as much.

"Isn't that Friend-of-Barf-Face sitting next to her?" said another kid.

"It must be. No one else would be brave enough to sit so close to a Barf-Machine," said Hadley, giggling.

I was glad when someone started singing "Ninety-nine Bottles of Pop." Other kids joined in. Soon we could not hear Hadley anymore.

As soon as the bus stopped, Hannie and I raced off and into Ms. Colman's class.

Nancy's bus had come earlier. She was sitting at her desk. She and Hannie sit all the way at the back of the room. I used to sit there with them. Then I got my glasses and Ms. Colman moved me to the front of the room. She said I could see better there.

"Hi," said Nancy. "How was the bus this morning?"

Before I had a chance to answer, Ms. Colman walked in.

"Please take your seats, everyone," she said.

24

I walked to the front of the room. I sit between two other glasses-wearers. They are Natalie Springer and Ricky Torres. (Ricky is my pretend husband. We got married on the playground at recess one afternoon.)

"Karen, would you like to take attendance this morning?" asked Ms. Colman.

"Yes!" I replied. Taking attendance is very cool.

I stood by Ms. Colman's desk. I looked around the room and checked off the names of the kids I saw. Hannie and Nancy. Check, check. Natalie and Ricky. Check, check. I saw Pamela Harding, my best enemy. Check. And I saw Pamela's best buddies, Leslie Morris and Jannie Gilbert. Check, check. Addie Sydney had just rolled into the room in her wheelchair. Check. There was Audrey Green. She tried to be my twin once, but we could not fool anyone. Check. The real twins, Terri and Tammy Barkan were there. Check, check. Hank Reubens and Chris Lamar were there.

Check, check. At first I did not see Bobby Gianelli, the sometimes bully. Then he popped up from under his desk. He must have been tying his shoe. Check.

I kept looking around and checking off names. Finally I said, "Everyone is here today."

"That is good because I need everyone's help," replied Ms. Colman. "In a couple of weeks we will take part in the school's Fall Festival. We will work to raise money to buy new books for our school library."

"What will we do to raise money?" asked Addie.

"That is where I need your help," said Ms. Colman. "Does anyone have any ideas?"

I am usually very good at coming up with ideas. My hand shot up.

"We could paint pictures and sell them," I said. "We could charge a dollar to clean classrooms. We could tell fortunes. We could . . ."

"Thank you, Karen. Those are all very

good suggestions. Maybe someone else has some, too. Your homework will be to think more about the festival and write down your ideas for raising money."

This was a very good homework assignment. I was glad I had a lot of paper at home. I just knew I would have more ideas.

Something Squishy

At recess, the Three Musketeers made up a cheer to keep my spirits up for the bus ride home.

Hannie and I sang it on the way to the bus after school.

"We are stick-together-girls,
Any-kind-of-weather-girls.
We are the Three Musketeers. Hooray!"

When we got on the bus, Hannie slipped

into the same seat she had in the morning. I sat down next to her. In two seconds, I popped up like a jack-in-the-box.

"Eww!" I cried. Something felt squishy underneath me. I looked down at my seat. I could hear the kids laughing at the back of the bus.

"Did you get our present, Barf-Face?" called Hadley.

The bus was pretty dark. But I could see a pile of something sickening and barflike on the seat. It was all over the back of my jean skirt, too.

"Do not worry," said Hannie. "It is just soggy cereal."

She helped me wipe off the seat with our leftover lunch napkins. Hadley and her pals were laughing and calling me names the whole time.

I knew they wanted me to cry. But I did not. Not for one whole minute. Not one tear.

I waited until I got home. I ran up to my

room and closed the door. I pulled off my jean skirt and put on clean leggings. Then I flomped down on the bed and cried and cried.

"Oh, Moosie," I said through my tears. "The big kids on the bus are being so mean to me. And all because I was nervous and got sick on the bus."

Moosie gave me a great big hug. I decided that Moosie was the only one I was going to tell. I did not want anyone feeling sorry for me. I did not want anyone to think I was a baby.

"Thank you, Moosie," I said. "I feel much better."

I washed my face. I was about to start my homework when Elizabeth called me to dinner.

I went downstairs with my notebook and pencil.

"Attention, everyone," I said in between bites of spaghetti. "We are having a Fall Festival at school. We need to find ways to raise money to buy books. Does anyone have any ideas?"

"A bake sale is always nice," said Nannie. "I could help you make cookies and cakes."

"That is a good idea, Nannie. Thank you," I said.

I wrote down Nannie's idea. I was starting to feel like my teacher, Ms. Colman.

"Does anyone else have an idea?" I said. Then I added, "Please raise your hand if you do."

"Hey, this is not school," said David Michael.

"Oh, all right," I said. "Do you have an idea?"

"You could have a game booth and sell tickets," said David Michael.

"Thank you. I will write that down," I replied.

" 'Tory time?" said Emily.

I think Emily was asking to hear a story.

But I made believe she was making a suggestion.

"Very good, Emily. We can charge a nickel a story," I replied.

By the time I finished dinner, I had two pages of ideas. Ms. Colman was going to be very happy.

Crybaby

There were green, gloopy globs on my ceiling. They were dripping onto the floor of my room.

In my head, I heard a voice say, "Glob-Face!"

I sat up in my bed. I looked all around. No one was there. I looked at the ceiling. It was clean and white.

"Oh, Moosie! I just had a terrible nightmare," I said.

I held Moosie in my arms. Soon I fell

asleep again. The next thing I knew the sun was shining in my window.

It was Wednesday morning. I got out of bed. But I did not get dressed. I went to the kitchen in my pajamas.

"Karen, honey, are you all right?" asked Elizabeth.

"I have a very bad stomachache," I said. "I am too sick to go to school."

"Let me see if you have a fever," said Daddy.

He touched my cheeks and my forehead.

"You do not feel warm," Daddy said. "Are you sure you can't make it to school today?"

"I am sure. I am afraid I will be sick on the bus again," I said.

"Don't you want to tell Ms. Colman all your good ideas for the Fall Festival?" said Elizabeth.

"Yes. But maybe I could call her," I said.

"Do you really and truly feel sick, Karen?" asked Daddy.

"Not really and truly. At least not now.

But I am really and truly afraid I will get sick on the bus. It is very bouncy," I said.

"Try it again this morning," said Elizabeth. "We think that would be best."

I got dressed and ate a tiny breakfast. That way I would only be a little sick.

When the bus pulled up, Hannie and I headed for our seats. But Hannie's seat was already taken. Meanie Hadley was sitting there.

There were other big kids up front, too. They were sitting in every other seat. Hannie and I could not find two empty seats together.

"Now what, Barf-Face? You can't sit next to your buddy, can you?" said one of the boys.

I could feel my eyes filling up with tears.

I will *not* cry, I will *not* cry, I told myself.

"I hope Barf-Face does not sit next to me," said Hadley. "I left my Barf-Coat home."

That did it. The tears spilled over. They

rolled down my cheeks. I was crying in front of everyone.

"Crybaby, crybaby, better dry your eyes, baby!" sang the big kids.

I was still crying a little bit when I walked into Ms. Colman's room. I was glad Ms. Colman was not there yet. I would have been embarrassed if she saw me crying, too.

"What happened?" asked Nancy.

Hannie and I took turns telling Nancy what the mean kids did.

"And they called me a crybaby," I said.

"That is *awful*," said Nancy. "I do not have that trouble. Bully Bobby protects me from the big kids."

I wished someone were on my bus to protect me. I wished I could bring Sam and Charlie. They would not let those kids be mean to me. They would not let them call me Barf-Face and crybaby.

Cake Walk

There was no more time for crying. I had important work to do.

Ms. Colman needed our ideas for the Fall Festival. When it was my turn, I stood up and read my list to the class. I had more ideas than anyone.

"Thank you for your ideas," said Ms. Colman. "I noticed that several of you suggested a bake sale. There is a special kind of bake sale you might like. It is called a Cake Walk. Does anyone know what a Cake Walk is?"

My hand shot up. I knew everything about Cake Walks. Kristy had one at her school last year.

"Will you explain it to us, Karen?" said Ms. Colman.

"Sure," I said. "You paint a big circle on the ground. You draw lines inside so it looks like a pie. You number the slices of pie. I will show you."

I went up to the blackboard and drew a picture. I felt gigundoly important.

"This is how you play the game," I said. "There is music playing. The kids walk around inside the circle. When the music stops, the kids stop walking. Someone calls out a number. Whoever is standing in the slice with that number wins. The prize is a wonderful cake. Any questions?"

There were no questions. I was turning into a very excellent teacher.

"Thank you, Karen. That was very helpful," said Ms. Colman.

The class voted. We decided that a Cake Walk was the best idea of all. We could charge a dollar a turn to play. We would make so much money. We could buy a whole library of books!

It was time for our math lesson. But first I had to think about the cake Nannie and I would make. What kind should it be? A wedding cake? A birthday cake? No. Those were ordinary. I wanted to make something really special.

A circus cake! I was the ringmaster in my summer circus camp. So I knew everything about the circus.

Hurry, hurry, hurry! Step right up for the greatest cake on earth.

Meanies

"See you tomorrow!" I called to Nancy.

I was in a happy mood when I left school on Wednesday. I had a very good plan for my circus cake. And I was the winner of our class spelling bee. (I am an excellent speller. That is E-X-C-E-L-L-E-N-T.)

Hannie and I walked to the bus stop together. I was in such a good mood, I did not think the ride home would bother me one bit.

I was wrong. As soon as I got on the bus, Hadley tripped me.

When I tripped, I dropped my notebook. The big kids got it and took it to the back of the bus. They played "Hot Potato" with it.

I wished the bus driver would help me. But he was too busy watching the road.

"Give my notebook back," I said.

"Make us," said Hadley.

I could not make them. So I started to cry again.

"Crybaby, crybaby, better dry your eyes, baby!" sang the big kids.

They gave back my notebook before I got off the bus. The page with my circus cake picture was torn down the middle.

I wiped my face carefully before I walked into my house. I did not want anyone to know I was a crybaby.

"Hi, honey," said Nannie. "How was school today?"

"School was fun," I said.

I was glad she did not ask about the bus ride home.

On Thursday Hannie picked me up at the big house. We walked to the bus stop together.

"They will get tired of being meanies," said Hannie.

"I hope so," I said.

But they did not get tired of being meanies on Thursday morning.

Hadley put an ice cube down my shirt. While Hannie was helping me get it out, another kid put one down Hannie's shirt.

"Baby one and baby two, stick together just like glue," sang Hadley.

That afternoon the big kids did not do one bad thing the whole way home. I could not believe it.

"You see. I told you they would get tired of being meanies," said Hannie.

I thought Hannie was right until we tried getting up. We could not. We were stuck to our seats!

"Boo-hoo, stuck with glue!" sang the kids from the back.

I had to pull hard to get off the seat. A little bit of my navy blue leggings was left behind.

Hannie and I ran off the bus and down the street.

"T.G.I.F.!" said Hannie. (That means Thank Goodness It's Friday.)

Only one more day until the weekend. "T.D.W.H.!" I said.

"What is that?" asked Hannie.

"Two Days Without Hadley!" I replied.

We ran the whole way home. I was never so happy to see my house. I waved to Hannie and went inside.

Hot Chili Sandwich

"Karen, you have hardly touched your dinner," said Nannie. "Are you okay?"

"I am not very hungry," I said.

Friday night dinners are usually my favorite. Especially when everyone is home. Sometimes Kristy has to leave early for a baby-sitting job. Sometimes Sam or Charlie leave early to meet their friends. But tonight everyone was there.

I wanted to have fun. But I could not. I was too busy thinking about Hadley and the bus.

I did not have much fun after dinner either.

"Do you want to play 'Go Fish'?" asked David Michael.

"No thanks," I replied.

"Do you want to watch TV with me?" asked Andrew.

"No thanks," I said.

" 'Tory time?" asked Emily.

"Not tonight," I said.

"You are no fun," said Andrew.

"You are right," I said.

I went up to my room. I found a book called *Bully Trouble* on my shelf. It is about a mean boy who bullies two little kids. But the little kids get back at the boy. They trick him into eating a hot chili sandwich. I liked that story.

I went to sleep thinking about Hadley Smith. I dreamed that I was going to trick her into eating a hot chili sandwich. But the dream turned into a nightmare. Hadley found out about the trick and made me eat the sandwich instead.

46

I woke up very thirsty.

On Saturday night I dreamed *all* the kids on the bus were Hadley Smith. Everywhere I looked there were meanie Hadleys. That was my worst nightmare ever.

By the time I woke up on Monday morning, I had a plan.

"I am not going to ride the bus today," I told Hannie on the way to the bus stop. "I am going to walk to school instead."

"Are you sure, Karen? I don't think it is such a good idea," said Hannie.

"Riding the bus is a much worse idea," I replied.

When we got to the bus stop, I left Hannie and turned the corner. I did not want to go the same way as the bus. I did not want anyone to see me.

I walked and walked. I walked and walked. By the time I got to school, I was very late.

"I am glad to see you, Karen," said Ms. Colman. "Do you have a note from home explaining why you are late?"

"I will bring it tomorrow," I replied.

After school, I walked Hannie to the bus stop again.

"Are you going to ride home?" asked Hannie.

"No way. I am not getting on that bus. I am going to run home. That way I will not be too late," I said.

I tied the laces on my sneakers. I tugged my knapsack straps tight.

"On my mark, get set, go!" I said to myself.

And I ran all the way home.

I Hate This Bus

I woke up extra early Tuesday morning. I was going to walk to school again. I did not want to be late two days in a row. Especially since I did not have a letter explaining why I was late the day before.

Plink! Plink-plink-plink! Uh-oh. I looked out my window. It was raining hard. I did not care. I was still going to walk to school.

After breakfast, I got dressed. Then I put on my yellow boots and raincoat. I found my cats and dogs umbrella in my closet. There were six cats and six dogs on it. I had a name for every one of them. Now I would have lots of company on my walk.

"Ready, everyone?" I asked.

I pretended there was lots of barking and meowing. That meant they were ready for our walk to school.

I slipped downstairs. I was almost out the door when Nannie stopped me.

"Aren't you leaving very early this morning?" she said.

"I think the bus comes early when it is raining," I replied.

"Well, you almost forgot your lunch," said Nannie. She tucked it into my knapsack.

"Thank you, Nannie," I said.

I walked down the block.

"Good-bye forever, Hadley Smith!" I said when I passed the bus stop.

I walked and walked. I walked and walked.

Suddenly I heard a car horn honking. The horn sounded familiar.

I turned around and saw a station wagon. It looked familiar, too.

"Karen, what *are* you doing?" called Daddy. "Please get into the car this minute."

I forgot that Daddy drove to work this way. I could see he was worried.

"What is wrong, Karen?" asked Daddy. "Why are you walking to school instead of taking the bus?"

"I hate riding that bus," I said.

"What is the matter with it?" asked Daddy.

I did not want to tell Daddy that the big kids were bothering me.

"I just do not like it," I said.

"Well, I am sorry, Karen," said Daddy. "You will have to ride the bus from now on."

Daddy drove me to school. He stopped to talk to Ms. Colman.

"Please be sure Karen gets on the bus this afternoon. I do not want her walking home alone. It is not safe," said Daddy.

After school, Ms. Colman walked me to the bus stop. She watched me get on. She stayed until the doors closed and the bus drove away.

I was trapped.

"Hey, look. Barf-Face is back," called Hadley. "Where have you been? We missed you so, so much."

"So did our little friend," said another big kid.

He tossed something in my lap. It was green and wiggly, with lots of legs.

I jumped up and screamed. The wiggly thing fell off my lap. It was a green rubber spider.

The big kids were all laughing.

"Along came a spider. He sat down beside her. He scared Little Barf-Face away!" called Hadley.

I really did hate this bus.

Baby, Baby!

It was Wednesday morning. Daddy wanted to walk me to the bus stop.

"I can get on the bus myself, Daddy. Really I can. And I will. I promise," I said.

"I am going with you, Karen," said Daddy. "I want to have a word with the bus driver."

I did not know what good that would do. The bus driver never seemed to notice what was going on. Maybe that was a good thing. At least the driver would not tell

Daddy how the big kids were teasing me.

"Hello, Hannie," said Daddy when we got to the bus stop.

"Hi, Mr. Brewer," said Hannie. She turned and gave me a "What-is-going-on?" look.

The other kids were not joking around the way they usually did. That is because a Grown-up was there. *My* Grown-up. I was so embarrassed.

"Here comes the bus!" said Linny. (He said that every morning.)

I climbed onto the bus. I turned to Daddy.

"You are not going to come on, are you? You can talk to the driver from there, right?" I said.

"No," said Daddy. "I am coming up."

Omigosh! Daddy climbed right *onto* the bus. There was suddenly a lot of whispering at the back of the bus. And giggling, too.

"I would like you to keep an eye on my

daughter, Karen," said Daddy. "She has been feeling a little uncomfortable on the bus."

"Sure. No problem," said the driver. "By the way, which one is Karen? Karen, can you raise your hand?"

I held my hand up a teeny, tiny bit. I could hear the giggling at the back of the bus getting louder and louder.

" 'Bye, Karen," said Daddy. "Have a good ride to school."

As soon as the doors closed, the big kids started teasing me.

"Is there a Karen on the bus?" said Hadley. "I don't think so. But we do have a Barf-Face!"

"Barf-Face can't get on the bus without her daddy," said another kid. "What a little baby!"

"I think she needs a rattle," said Hadley.

Then they all sang, *"Baby, baby, stick your head in gravy! Wash it off in bubble gum and send it to the Navy!"*

When I got to school, I could not think about my work. All I could think about was the bus ride home.

"Karen, are you all right?" asked Ms. Colman. "You do not seem to be paying attention today."

"Sorry," I said.

At recess, I sat with Hannie and Nancy at the jungle gym on the playground.

"What are you going to do?" asked Nancy. "You know they are going to be mean again this afternoon."

"Maybe I will put cotton in my ears. Then I will not have to listen to them," I replied.

But at the end of the day, something wonderful happened. Ms. Colman was not able to walk me to the bus.

"I am sorry, Karen. I have a meeting to go to this afternoon. Will you be okay getting on the bus by yourself?" said Ms. Colman.

"Oh, yes," I replied. "I will be fine."

I will be more than fine, I thought. I will

be great! I walked to the bus stop in case someone was watching. Then I slipped away and ran all the way home.

I got to my block just as the bus was pulling up.

I decided that I was never going to ride that bus again.

No More Bus, Yippee!

When I woke up Thursday morning, I made an Important Announcement.

"I am not going to ride that bus," I said to Moosie.

I went to the bathroom to wash my face and brush my teeth.

"I am not going to ride that bus," I said to my toothbrush.

I said it to my cereal. I said it to my glass of orange juice. Finally I said it to Daddy and Elizabeth.

"Don't you want to go to school?" asked Elizabeth.

"Oh, yes. I want to go to school. I just do not want to ride the bus anymore," I said.

"We cannot let you walk to school again," said Daddy. "It is too far."

Nannie was in the kitchen. She was giving Emily her breakfast.

"I would be happy to drive Karen to school," said Nannie. "Emily can come with us. She always enjoys going for a ride."

"Thank you, Nannie! Thank you!" I said. "Is it okay? Can Nannie drive me to school?"

Daddy and Elizabeth looked at each other.

"We will try it for awhile," said Daddy. "We will see how it goes."

I was so happy. I ate every bite of my breakfast. Then I called Hannie to tell her the good news.

"I hope you do not mind," I said.

"No. The big kids do not bother me when I am by myself," Hannie replied. "I am happy for you."

Nannie drove me to school in the Pink Clinker. I sat in the back with Emily. We played the whole way.

From then on, I had fun at school every day. That is because I was not worrying about the bus.

On the next Thursday we started to make the signs for our Cake Walk. I made up a very good sign. It was shaped like a cake. The words looked like they were written in icing. Here is what my sign looked like:

"That is wonderful," said Ms. Colman. "Have you decided what kind of cake you are going to bake?"

"I am going to bake a circus cake. It will be very beautiful," I said.

"I am sure it will be," said Ms. Colman. Then she added, "I am glad you are feeling better these days, Karen."

On the ride home with Nannie and Emily, we planned my circus cake.

"I would like it to be white with pink icing," I said. "Maybe it could have different colored sprinkles, too. The circus has lots of colors."

"Cowns?" said Emily.

"Clowns are a good idea," I said. "Nannie, do you think we could draw a clown face on the top of my cake?"

"Of course we can," Nannie replied.

A clown on my cake. No more bus. Yippee!

Mr. Wilson's Promise

It was a happy Saturday. Every day that I did not have to get on the bus was happy. I had not been on the bus for one whole week and two whole days.

I hurried out of bed and down to the kitchen.

"Hi," I said. "What is everybody doing today?"

Kristy had a baby-sitting job. Sam and Charlie were playing touch football with their friends. David Michael was meeting Linny. Even Andrew and Emily had plans.

Nannie and Elizabeth were taking them to buy shoes.

"I have some errands to do in town. Would you like to come with me?" said Daddy.

"Sure!" I replied. I love going to town with Daddy. Sometimes we stop to have lunch. Then I feel like a grown-up Lovely Lady.

"I would like to stop at the hardware store," said Daddy. "I need a few gardening tools."

Hardware stores are fun. The shelves are always filled with interesting things. Daddy went straight to the tools. I was going to look at the paints. I love all the different colors. On the way, I found a basket of tiny sponges. A sign said the sponges grew sixteen times bigger when wet. This was truly amazing.

The sponges were three for one dollar. I was wondering if Daddy wanted to buy some. Then guess who stopped right in front of me. It was my school bus driver.

"Hi. You are Karen, right? I have not seen you on my bus lately," he said.

"No, you have not," I replied. "I do not like your mean old bus."

"Why not?" asked the driver. He looked surprised. And a little worried, too.

"Every time I get on your bus, the big kids tease me. They are meanies," I said.

I told him everything that happened to me, starting with the very first day.

"And I will *never* get on that bus again!" I said.

"I am sorry, Karen. I did not know you were having such a hard time," said the bus driver. "I was so busy driving I did not know what was happening behind me. If you want to ride the bus again, I promise things will be different. I will make some changes."

Just then Daddy came over, carrying his basket of gardening tools.

"Hello, Mr. Brewer. I don't know if you

remember me. I am Jack Wilson, Karen's school bus driver," he said. Mr. Wilson shook Daddy's hand.

"We started driving Karen to school," said Daddy. "She was not happy on the bus."

"Yes, Karen told me," said Mr. Wilson. "I promised her I will make some changes. Do you think I could get your phone number? I will call to invite Karen back on my bus very soon."

Daddy gave Mr. Wilson our phone number. I wondered if Mr. Wilson would keep his promise. I was not too sure.

The Circus Cake

There was flour and sugar everywhere. Most of it was in the bowl where it belonged. The rest of it was on the table, on my fingers, and in my hair.

It was Friday afternoon. Tomorrow was the Fall Festival. Nannie and I were in the kitchen baking our cake.

"It says in the cookbook that we have to beat in three eggs," I said.

"That sounds like a good job for you," said Nannie. "I will turn on the oven."

We finished making the batter. Then we

poured it into three pans and put it in the oven.

While it was baking we made French Cream Filling to put between the layers. We made Fluffy Pink Frosting to spread on top.

Suddenly everyone started coming into the kitchen. That is because the cake smelled so delicious.

"That smells great," said Sam. "Will it be ready soon?"

"It is not for us. It is for my Fall Festival tomorrow," I said.

"Can I have some frosting?" said David Michael.

"No way!" I said. "We need it for the cake."

Emily came in dragging her teddy bear behind her.

"Candy for Teddy?" she said.

"Nannie, help!!" I cried.

"All right, everyone please leave the kitchen. Karen and I have work to do," said Nannie.

"That is right. I am an important baker.

I must have privacy when working," I said.

When the cake was baked and cooled, Nannie and I piled the filling between the layers. Then we spread the frosting and put on colored sprinkles.

"Is it time to make the clown, Nannie?" I asked.

"It is time," Nannie replied.

We had four tubes of colored frosting. It took a long time to make the perfect circus clown. I squeezed on red frosting for the clown's nose and mouth and cheeks. I squeezed on blue for the eyes. I squeezed on yellow hair. I trimmed the cake with green squiggles.

When it was done, Nannie clapped for my cake.

"It is spectacular," said Nannie. "You should be very proud."

It really was the most beautiful cake ever. It looked like a real bakery shop cake.

I was busy admiring my cake when the phone rang.

"Karen, it is for you," said Elizabeth.

I washed my hands. (I did not think any-one wanted a frosted telephone.)

"Hello?" I said.

"This is Jack Wilson, your bus driver," said the voice at the other end. "I have worked out plans for changes on the bus. If you will ride the bus on Monday, I think you will be pleased."

"I do not know if I want to ride the bus again," I said.

"I promise that if there is any teasing I will stop the bus," said Mr. Wilson. "And that is only one part of my plan. If you ride the bus, you will be surprised to see what else I have done. Will you ride with us on Monday?"

"I will have to think about it," I said.

"Well, I hope I will see you," said Mr. Wilson.

I thanked Mr. Wilson and hung up the phone. I had some serious thinking to do.

But I would start thinking later. It was time to take a picture of my beautiful circus cake.

Setting Up

Yippee! It was Saturday. The Fall Festival would begin at noon.

Ms. Colman's class was going to meet at school at ten o'clock to set up.

Daddy drove Hannie, me, and my circus cake to school.

"Please watch out for bumps, Daddy," I said. "I do not want the cake to get ruined."

"Karen! Hannie! We are over here," called Nancy.

It was a sunny day, so the festival was being held out on the playground.

"Now that we are all together, we can make our Cake Walk circle," said Ms. Colman. "I drew the outline and numbers on the ground this morning with chalk. Now we need to cover the chalk with masking tape."

Making the Cake Walk game was gigundoly fun. I love getting down on the ground and crawling around. Only I did not watch where I was going. I bumped heads with Bobby the Bully.

"Hey, watch out!" I started to shout. Then I remembered how he protected Nancy from the big kids on the bus.

"Sorry I bumped into you, Bobby," I said.

"That is okay," said Bobby. (Sometimes he can be nice.)

Pamela Harding, my best enemy, was hogging the tape. But we were having too much fun to fuss. I did not yell or anything. I just waited my turn.

When we finished, our Cake Walk circle looked just like the picture I drew on the blackboard. We used the cake signs we made in class. We hung them over a long table covered with red crepe paper. We lined the cakes up in their boxes. Our booth was finished.

"Feel free to walk around and look at the other booths," said Ms. Colman. "We will meet back here a few minutes before noon."

I walked around the playground with Hannie and Nancy. We saw lots of games we wanted to play.

"Look!" I said. "There is Hadley Smith. Her class has the dunking booth. I wonder if you-know-who will take a turn in the dunking seat."

Hannie and Nancy each got big grins on their faces. But I am sure I had the biggest grin of all.

The sign said twenty-five cents a turn. I had three dollars to spend. I did the math problem in my head.

"There are twelve quarters in three dollars," I said. "If Hadley Smith sits in that seat, I will have twelve chances to dunk her."

Fall Festival

The playground was filling up with guests. Both my families were there. I love when my two families get together. For a while I can pretend I have one great, big family. Then instead of being Karen Two-Two, I am just plain Karen for a day.

"Karen, your cake is gorgeous," said Mommy. "Did you make that all by yourself?"

"Nannie helped a little with the baking. But the clown is all mine," I said.

I could hear people talking about my cake

when they walked by it. They were all saying nice things. Maybe they would try extra hard to win it because it was so beautiful.

At noon, our principal rang a bell and made a little speech.

"Welcome to our Fall Festival," she said. "We are trying to raise money to buy new books for our school library. We appreciate your coming here today to help us out. Have a wonderful time everybody."

The students and guests all started walking around looking for games to play and things to buy. I had the first shift at our booth. It was my job to start and stop the music. This was a very important thing to do.

Ms. Colman asked Natalie to hold up her cake. It was drooping a little to one side. But that was no surprise. Natalie's socks are always drooping, too.

Addie was the announcer.

"Who would like a chance to win this tasty chocolate cake?" she asked.

Four kids and two grown-ups gave Ricky

one dollar each. He put the six dollars in the class money box.

"All right, listen up!" I called. "The Cake Walk is about to begin."

I pressed the start button on the tape recorder. The song was "All Around the Mulberry Bush."

I let it play a little while, then pressed the stop button.

"Everyone freeze!" I called.

Hannie picked a number from our number box.

"The winning number is ten!" said Hannie.

"I won! I won!" said Liddie Yuan.

Natalie handed Liddie the chocolate cake.

"I hope you enjoy it," said Natalie.

Audrey's strawberry shortcake was next. Five people played the game.

Nine people played the game to win Ricky's brownie cake.

"Karen, your cake is next," said Ms. Colman.

I held it up so everyone could see it.

"Who would like a chance to win this beautiful circus cake?" said Addie.

I could hardly believe it. Eleven kids and four grown-ups paid one dollar each to win my cake. That made fifteen dollars!

The winner was a lady I did not know.

"My grandchildren will love this!" she said.

After our cakes were sold, the Three Musketeers walked around the festival together.

We bought hot dogs and juice. I played water-balloon basketball and won a pinwheel. We had our fortunes told. My fortune said *There is a happy surprise in store for you soon*.

We were about to play Pin the Tail on the Dinosaur. But there were shouts coming from the fifth-graders' dunking booth. I turned to see what all the noise was about.

Guess who was in the dunking seat. Miss Hadley Smith.

Splash!

"Step right up and dunk a fifth-grader," called a boy in Hadley's class. "Three tries for twenty-five cents."

I hurried to get in line. I had to dunk Hadley. I just *had* to.

"Here is my quarter," I said when my turn came.

Suddenly there was a crowd at the dunking booth. It was mostly kids from the bus. There was lots of giggling and whispering all around me.

The boy running the booth gave me three

softballs. He pointed to a target with colored circles.

"All you have to do is hit the big red circle in the center," he said.

I looked at Hadley. She stuck her tongue out at me. I did not have to stick my tongue out at her. That is because I had three balls in my hand. As soon as I threw one of them right, Hadley would be a silly-soggy fifth-grader.

I pulled my arm back. I aimed for the red circle. I threw the ball. Oops. I missed the red circle and hit the yellow one.

I tried again with the second ball. Oops. I missed the red circle and hit the blue one.

On the last try, I hit the yellow circle again.

I could still hear the kids cheering. And do you know what? They were cheering for *me*.

"Go, Karen!" called one of the little kids. "Do not give up."

"Dunk her in the water!" called a first-grader.

"I want to try again," I said to the boy.

I handed over another quarter. The boy handed me three more balls.

I threw the first ball. I missed the red circle and the blue one. Boo and bullfrogs.

"Go, Karen, go!" called Nancy.

"Think about the bus rides," called Hannie.

That did it. I pulled back my arm. I looked straight at the red circle. I threw the ball.

I did it! I hit the red circle!

SPLASH! Hadley went down in the tub of water.

The kids were laughing and cheering.

"So there, Miss Hadley Smith," I said.

Hadley stood up. She was soaked. Her cheeks were red. She was just a silly-soggy fifth-grader. Hadley Smith did not look like such a big shot now.

I was ready to ride the bus on Monday.

Mr. Wilson's Surprise

When I woke up on Monday morning I felt one little butterfly in my stomach.

"I am *not* going to be scared," I said to Moosie.

But by the time I finished breakfast, I felt two little butterflies in my stomach.

I called Hannie.

"Hi," I said. "Can I walk to the bus stop with you this morning?"

Hannie and I held hands the whole way. When we got to the bus stop, all the kids were really happy to see me.

"Way to go, Karen," said one kid. "You will not have to worry about Hadley any more."

I was not so sure.

"Here comes the bus!" called Linny.

Linny got on first. I climbed on right behind him.

The first thing I did was look for Hadley at the back of the bus. I did not see her there. I looked all around.

Guess where Hadley was sitting. Right in the very first seat. That was Mr. Wilson's surprise. The other big kids were up front, too. I knew that Mr. Wilson could keep an eye on them there. He would make sure they did not make any more trouble.

Mr. Wilson smiled at me. Hadley turned and looked the other way.

"Your seat is at the back of the bus now, Karen," Mr. Wilson said. "I have assigned seats to all my riders. No one is allowed to change."

I walked with Hannie to the back of the bus.

"It is fun being back here," said Hannie. "It is like it used to be when we sat at the back of Ms. Colman's class."

"You are right," I said. "I wish Nancy were here, too. We will invite her to stay over one night. Then the Three Musketeers can ride to school together."

"Good idea," said Hannie. She thought for a moment. "Guess what. When we get to school today, we will find out how much money we made at the Fall Festival. I think we made a lot."

"We will be able to buy a lot of new books for our library," I said. "I have an idea. We can make a list of the books we think they should buy. We will give it to Ms. Colman when we get to school."

I took out my notebook and a pencil. We wrote down the names of our favorite books. Some of the other kids told us books they liked, too.

It was a very good bus ride. There were no butterflies in my stomach. Nobody bothered us the whole way.

On the way out, I stopped to thank Mr. Wilson.

"I am going to like riding on your bus from now on," I said.

"I am very glad, Karen," said Mr. Wilson. "That is the way it should be."

I waved good-bye to Mr. Wilson and skipped all the way into school.

About the Author

ANN M. MARTIN lives in New York City and loves animals, especially cats. She has two cats of her own, Mouse and Rosie.

Other books by Ann M. Martin that you might enjoy are *Stage Fright*; *Me and Katie (the Pest)*; and the books in *The Baby-sitters Club* series.

Ann likes ice cream and *I Love Lucy*. And she has her own little sister, whose name is Jane.

Little Sister

Don't miss #54

KAREN'S CANDY

"Oh, no! Look!"

Nancy and Hannie looked where I was pointing. There were our enemies. They were crowded around Pamela's desk. And they were looking at forms and envelopes. The forms and envelopes were from Polly's Fine Candy.

"They are going to sell candy, too!" cried Nancy.

"Shhh!" I hissed. But I was too late. Pamela had heard her. She looked back at us.

"Are *you* selling candy?" she asked.

"Yes. Are you?" (Pamela nodded.) "Where?" I asked.

"Why do you care?" replied Pamela.

I thought for a moment. "I guess I do not care — since we are going to sell more candy than you are."

88888888 LITTLE 🍎 APPLE 88888888

BABY·SITTERS

Little Sister™

by Ann M. Martin, author of *The Baby-sitters Club* ®

❑	MQ44300-3	#1	Karen's Witch	$2.95
❑	MQ44259-7	#2	Karen's Roller Skates	$2.95
❑	MQ44299-7	#3	Karen's Worst Day	$2.95
❑	MQ44264-3	#4	Karen's Kittycat Club	$2.95
❑	MQ44258-9	#5	Karen's School Picture	$2.95
❑	MQ44298-8	#6	Karen's Little Sister	$2.95
❑	MQ44257-0	#7	Karen's Birthday	$2.95
❑	MQ42670-2	#8	Karen's Haircut	$2.95
❑	MQ43652-X	#9	Karen's Sleepover	$2.95
❑	MQ43651-1	#10	Karen's Grandmothers	$2.95
❑	MQ43650-3	#11	Karen's Prize	$2.95
❑	MQ43649-X	#12	Karen's Ghost	$2.95
❑	MQ43648-1	#13	Karen's Surprise	$2.75
❑	MQ43646-5	#14	Karen's New Year	$2.75
❑	MQ43645-7	#15	Karen's in Love	$2.75
❑	MQ43644-9	#16	Karen's Goldfish	$2.75
❑	MQ43643-0	#17	Karen's Brothers	$2.75
❑	MQ43642-2	#18	Karen's Home-Run	$2.75
❑	MQ43641-4	#19	Karen's Good-Bye	$2.95
❑	MQ44823-4	#20	Karen's Carnival	$2.75
❑	MQ44824-2	#21	Karen's New Teacher	$2.95
❑	MQ44833-1	#22	Karen's Little Witch	$2.95
❑	MQ44832-3	#23	Karen's Doll	$2.95
❑	MQ44859-5	#24	Karen's School Trip	$2.95
❑	MQ44831-5	#25	Karen's Pen Pal	$2.95
❑	MQ44830-7	#26	Karen's Ducklings	$2.75
❑	MQ44829-3	#27	Karen's Big Joke	$2.95
❑	MQ44828-5	#28	Karen's Tea Party	$2.95

More Titles... ➡

Now THE BABY-SITTERS CLUB.

★ is a Video Club too! ★

JOIN TODAY—

- Save $5.00 on your first video!
- 10-day FREE examination-before-you-keep policy!
- New video adventure every other month!
- Never an obligation to buy anything!

Now you can play back the adventures of America's favorite girls whenever you like. Share them with your friends too.

Just pop a tape into a VCR and watch *Claudia and the Mystery of the Secret Passage* or view *Mary Anne and the Brunettes, The Baby-sitters and the Boy Sitters, Dawn Saves the Trees* or any of the girls' many exciting, fun-packed adventures.

Don't miss this chance to actually see and hear Kristy, Stacey, Mallory, Jessi and the others in this new video series. Full details below.

■ ■ ■ CUT OUT AND MAIL TODAY! ■ ■ ■

MAIL TO: Baby-sitters Video Club • P.O. Box 30628 • Tampa, FL 33630-0628

Please enroll me as a member of the Baby-sitters Video Club and send me the first video, *Mary Anne and the Brunettes* for only $9.95 plus $2.50 shipping and handling. I will then receive other video adventures—one approximately every other month—at the regular price of $14.95 plus $2.50 shipping/handling each for a 10-day FREE examination. There is never any obligation to buy anything.

NAME	PLEASE PRINT
ADDRESS	APT.
CITY	
STATE	ZIP
BIRTH DATE	
( )	
AREA CODE	DAYTIME PHONE NUMBER

CHECK ONE:
☐ I enclose $9.95 plus $2.50 shipping/handling.
☐ Charge to my card: ☐ VISA ☐ MASTERCARD ☐ AMEX

Card number_____   Expiration Date_____

Parent's signature:_____   9AP ⑤⑤

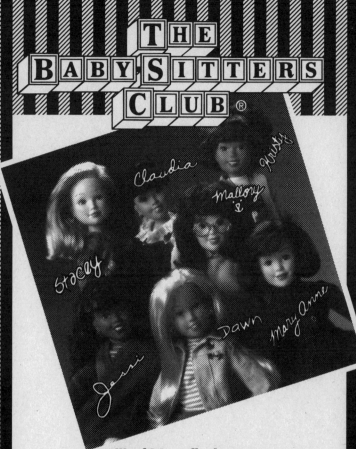

THE BABY-SITTERS CLUB ®

Stacey · Claudia · Kristy · Mallory · Jessi · Dawn · Mary Anne

Wow! It's really them—
the new Baby-sitters Club dolls!

Your favorite Baby-sitters Club characters have come to life in these
beautiful collector dolls. Each doll wears her own unique clothes and jewelry.
They look just like the girls you have imagined! The dolls also come with their own
individual stories in special edition booklets that you'll find nowhere else.

Look for the new Baby-sitters Club collection...
coming soon to a store near you!

Kenner®